MCSWEENEY'S BOOKS

THIS
SHAPE
WE'RE
IN

THIS
SHAPE
WE'RE
IN

---

by

JONATHAN
LETHEM

McSweeney's Books

Acknowpologies to David Gates and Franz Kafka

McSWEENEY'S BOOKS
429 Seventh Avenue
Brooklyn, NY 11215

Published in the United States by McSweeney's Books

McSWEENEY'S and colophon are registered trademarks
of McSweeney's, a privately held company with
wildly fluctuating resources.

First published in the United States by McSweeney's, 2001

Manufactured in Iceland by Oddi Printing

1   3   5   7   9   10   8   6   4   2

Library of Congress Cataloging-in-Publication Data
ISBN: 0-9703355-2-0

IT BEGAN when Balkan came into our burrow during cocktail hour and told us he had been in the eye. Earl and Lorna were sitting around sipping gin and tonics and watching me grill a hunk of proteinous rind which I'd marinated pretty nicely and was basting like a real pro and my immediate response was to tell Balkan to go to hell. Marianne offered him a drink and he took it with both hands like it was hot chocolate and went back to boasting about his extraordinary meander and the culture of the forelimbs and the things he'd witnessed peering through the eye: the inky depths of interstellar space (*his* words: *inky depths, interstellar space*). Balkan believed he dwelt in the liver or *seat of the soul* and I happened to know he was wrong, that in fact Balkan and his bunker of weirdos were dwelling in the rump—merely the seat. Balkan was the same age as my son Dennis, was an old pal of Dennis's, in fact. He wouldn't have known the liver from an amphitheater or an orgy and I could be pretty sure he'd been deceived about the eye as well: it wouldn't be the first time some priestly collective mounted a bogus eye and started preaching to deluded seekers and gullible militia types like Balkan about the wonders to be seen, the answers to be had.

But all I said was, "Which eye?"

"Which?"

That's right, kid, I thought, *bring this mystical shit into my burrow and drink up my liquor.* "Right, left, or third?"

"I don't know," said Balkan, hemming. "I just know it was an eye, Mr. F. Don't try to tell me it wasn't." Then: "There's a *third?*"

"Oh yeah," I said. "The visionary eye, looks into the face of God—and God's got his finger in his nostril, to the knuckle. In fact we're a booger, Balkan, hadn't word reached you?" In truth I'd only heard faint legends of a third eye myself—when Dennis was in kindergarten in the pizzle and he came home having played some children's game, chanting under his breath: *Third eye third eye watching me/third eye third eye it can see/third eye third eye set me free/my mother says to pick the very next one!* I yanked Dennis out of that school the next day and that was right about when Marianne and I decided to find our way out to the subburrows. And I knew fuckall about what any such alleged third eye looked out on. Such ignorance is what passed for bliss, those days.

"Don't be mean," said Marianne to me. "I'm sure it was an eye, Balkan, and probably a very important one. You know, we're just not that *interested* in space around here." Her words were a condescending veneer of charm stretched over a yawning gulf of boredom.

Then she asked: "Can I refresh anyone's drink?" It wasn't so much a question as a gesture in the barbecue Kabuki, signaling we should get off the topic and back to some more general jabber along the way to getting potted. There came various murmurs of satisfaction, a bowl of chips was passed around, and Earl asked Balkan a few polite questions about the stripes of rank on his shoulder and what they meant, though I knew he didn't give two hoots on a rusty trumpet.

I slivered off chunks of that marinated rind and put it in buns loaded up with onions and Balkan took one from me and wolfed it like a hunted thing. Poor bastard was malnourished physically and in other ways and I thought for the hundredth time *God Bless marriage, grilling, distilled spirits, and all else that distracts from wayward sons and wayward theories,* and it was while I was in the thick of this coarse, gratifying epiphany, I swear, that Balkan said, "I saw Dennis up there. He's a beggar in the eye."

Marianne, suddenly attentive, said: "What did you say?"

Balkan knew he had her attention now. "Dennis, your son, sure. He sits in the back of the eye and chants and says prayers for money."

Of course, this was what Balkan had come to say in the first place. It was absolutely like him to *bury the lead.*

"Oh, Balkan, why didn't you bring him back?" said Marianne.

"Don't listen to him," I said to Marianne. "He didn't see *anyone.* Balkan, get screwed." I stood from my chair as though to make a grab or throw a punch, but in fact I still had my drink in my hand, and only lurched.

"Maybe we ought to get going, folks," said Earl, though Lorna was still only halfway through her plate. Lorna nibbled nervously on her sandwich, eyes wide like a ferret.

"He's your son," said Marianne to me. She stepped up and plucked at my glass, which I fought for, causing half my lovely gin to slosh over my wrist and trickle onto my leg and into the astroturf.

"Christ, woman." I said it in my John Wayne voice, a joke which general mush-mouthedness caused to be completely lost if it had stood a snowball's chance in the first place. Still, I thought it pretty good-humored, given the waste of a cocktail.

"Henry," said Marianne. "Dennis needs you. He's your son."

"You ought to listen to Balkan," said Earl, thumping me on the shoulder. "You ought to go with him and bring him back."

"Ha! I ought to send Balkan back with a bill for services rendered. I gave that kid fourteen non-refundable years of reasonably adequate parenthood, under damned strained conditions. But we'd be assuming Balkan here could even blunder his way back to this so-called eye."

"Right with you, Captain," said Balkan, saluting me.

"Don't call me Captain!" I said. "Don't call me Dad or Captain or capsized or late for dinner!" Okay—so I was engaged in a lot of nervous riffing but neverthe-less striking a jocular note, if they could hear it.

They couldn't. Marianne in the relevant particular. She tore off her apron and flung it, straight upwards, where it weirdly hooked on our burrow's fluorescent ceiling fixture. Then she began to cry. "You drove him aw-aw-away—" were the words I heard in the teary, gasping mix.

"Oh, no," protested Balkan, out of his depth. "Dennis isn't *mad* at you and Mr. F—"

"No, he's just turned into a broken, abject beggar," sniffled Marianne. "Dennis couldn't stay mad at a fly—" The oddness of this thought seemed to slow her down, and she left it unfinished.

"It's okay, honey," said Lorna, who was over con-soling Marianne with an arm draped around her shoulders in a blink, making me look like a jerk for what I'd begun doing instead: fixing another cocktail.

I took it to Marianne once it was poured, figuring better late than etc., but paused behind the curtain of the hanging apron to level off the top with a sip which turned out to be half the glass, somewhat damaging my already-thin point. Marianne glared at me, then took it anyway and had a healthy slurp herself. Which seemed to right her ship rather quickly.

"You go find Dennis and bring him back," she said, eyes red and squinky like a mole's, but voice fiberglass-tough.

"No can do," I said. "Dennis is his own, um—" I lost a word here, and aggressively wrong ones pushed forward to take its place: his own *can-of-worms? Commanding officer? Best-case-scenario?* Then in place of any word I substituted a pratfall: losing my balance I grabbed for the apron and tugged down the fluorescent light fixture, bulb shattering against the grill and powdering the remaining cuts of rind with crystalline white dust. The women and Balkan shrieked and danced backwards and Earl, in some sort of sketchy volunteer-fireman impulse, doused the grill and the shattered fixture with his drink. It flared like Baked Alaska, then sizzled greasily and died.

"Wow," I said, gesturing at the strange scene on the grill. "What's for dinner? Looks like smoker's lung!" This came out more aggressive, less self-deprecating than I'd hoped. Balkan scraped at the wreckage on the floor of the burrow with the toe of his boot, and

I noticed for the first time that he was wearing a spur. I wondered if he even knew what it was for.

"Get out!" screamed Marianne. "Don't come back without Dennis!"

I reached for Marianne, meaning to hug her into silence but she gripped my arms at the shoulders and so we locked into a stiff tango. "Ur—hey!" We tilted and slid like a lopsided rockinghorse, and Balkan and Lorna scrambled away. Earl had already climbed up into the corridor, and was peering down into our burrow to follow the quote-unquote action.

"Let go of me, you lousy, drunken—" Marianne fished for a word here, came up with: "—clown!" I guess I'd already disqualified or preempted a bunch of other possible insults.

"Well at least I've got a job," I joked, meaning *clown,* but this just wasn't my day for getting punch-lines across. I suppose this one was a stretch in the first place, since clown would have been a step up from my current occupation: garbage hider for the subburrow. I basically spent my time sneaking into other parts of the shape—spleen, hind legs, etc.—and concealing our offal and eggshells under other people's shrubbery and mattresses.

Now my feet tangled in the legs of the grill, and Marianne and I went down. "Oh boy," I said. "Feels like maybe I broke something—"

"GET OUT NOW!" screamed Marianne.

"I THINK I WILL!" What a strong hand I had to play.

"YOU DO THAT!"

"HERE I GO AND DON'T COUNT ON ME COMING BACK! I MAY JUST TAKE UP CHANTING MYSELF!"

And so on—the long and the short of it, not that I remember all of the long, is that I found myself with Balkan in the tunnel above the lungs an hour later, having salvaged only the gin jar and my old service revolver before being expelled from the burrow in a hail of Marianne's alternated denunciations and importunings, the former roughly or even precisely deserved, the latter probably useless but driving my secretly fond and guilty heart onward, to quest through parts of the shape I'd wished never to see again in search of a son whose fate a rat's ass meant to me slightly more than. If it matters, I believed I was doing it all for Marianne. I loved Marianne. I never saw her again.

I nudged Balkan awake in the dark of the pew where we were hidden and asked him to pass me the sacramental wine we'd pilfered to follow the gin we'd worn out. Balkan lay sprawled across several knee-pillows, his fingers folded over the drum-tight bulge of his drink-swollen belly where his shirt had hitched up.

Before he'd passed out I'd prompted some nice ravings from him concerning the *inky depths*, etc. "The shape is an *intergenerational starship*," he said with immense pride and satisfaction at mastering the five-dollar word and its implications. "We just forgot, that's all. They sent us out to colonize another planet, and we just forgot. Oh, Mr. F, if you saw it you'd know. We've gotta get ready for the landing, I feel it coming, everybody feels it coming—" Now he murmured and handed me the chalice, returned to dozing. But the wine itself was exhausted, down to dregs, like the gin, like Balkan, everyone but me. I couldn't sleep. I was listening to various faint echoes and howls deep in the shape: running feet, some grinding or whirring machine, shouted commands, a distant ringing phone, one-sided moaning. The left lung is a cathedral, one of the largest open spaces in the shape, and noises are transmitted from every side and through every portal. It was a lung that breathed sound, it seemed to me as I huddled there. Balkan's snoring was the metronome for this soundscape's tired rehearsal of options—I didn't want to stay where I was and I didn't want to budge and I couldn't go crawling back to Marianne, not yet anyway. And if Dennis was actually to be found it was plain I would have to be both pilot and navigator, or bushwhacker and safari master, that Balkan was only dead weight and noncomic unrelief. My boy Dennis, and his pal Balkan, the fresh green troops

ended up, old whatsisname, the genius bartender—Highball? Could he have really been named Highball? Anyway, poor Highball's fate or how long it had been since the W.B.W., either one I didn't want to consider. The past is the religion I was raised in, but I don't practice religion.

These camouflage fetishists had two-thirds of the spine's width cordoned off and lit with flares. They searched us and impounded my revolver, then steered me and Balkan into what had been a nice little watering hole, to wait behind a few other hapless stragglers they'd rounded up for interrogation by their "chief officer," a kid barely older than Balkan with a pointy Custer mustache, a wannabe martinet. The only evidence of their HQ's previous incarnation was a shelf of dusty commemorative plates—dead young movie stars and presidents rendered in porcelain—above what had been a shelf full of exotic single malts. "Have you any orders?" he said and I couldn't really keep from saying, "Scotch, rocks." In fact I could see they had put old Highball's fabricator to depressingly pedantic use cranking out some pinkish goo that looked something like Spam, or possibly Oobleck. A couple of guys were eating the stuff out of bowls, while others were using scoops to direct it as it was pumped out and packing it into half-gallon containers like it was ice cream.

"We're headed for the eye, sir," said Balkan, nervously trying to cover my gaffe.

"Why are you calling him *sir?*" I said. "This isn't your, uh, unit, is it Balkan?"

Balkan blinked at me, then spoke to the beady-eyed officer. "Captain Farbur has been away from the field for some time. He asked me to escort him on a tour of recognizance."

I poked Balkan in the ribs. "Don't you mean *reconnaissance?*"

Balkan and the officer both blinked at that one.

"Maybe *pre*cognizance," I said, while I had them going. "We are looking for the *third* eye, right?"

This had an odd effect on the littlest soldier man, as though I'd said *"The password is 'the password'"* or *"These aren't the droids you're looking for."* He grabbed my hand and shook it again, then said in an intimate, confidential tone, "We've been getting some pretty intriguing reports from up around the third eye."

"Ah, *reports*," I said, raising my eyebrow. "From *precognizance?*"

"From various sources," he said defensively. "We've been in touch with Central Command."

"Central Command. Really. Congratulations. Central Command is not usually so—" I had to search for a decorous word here "—so *forthcoming*."

"Oh, they've been very *forthcoming*," boasted the little soldier, quite relieved that I appeared to credit his breakthrough.

"You should see it, Mr. F," said Balkan, blowing

our cover in his excitement, not that it apparently mattered. "They came through and put in these phones everywhere. The phones are bright red, that's how you know you've got a direct channel to Central Command."

"And *they* is exactly—who?" I asked.

The soldier and Balkan looked at one another, each insecure of their own theories about the phones, I guess.

"Central ... Command?" ventured Balkan at last, as though I'd be grading his test later.

The soldier nodded eager confirmation. Seemingly that was what he would have said too, if he'd found his tongue.

"Well, that's exciting," I said, though it wasn't anything remotely. The echolalic circularity of this exchange was only going to keep my mind off finding a drink for a very short time more. "I'm gonna have to get me one a them *bright red phones.*" I chuckled, and, though plainly bewildered, Balkan and the soldier took the cue and we all had a good hearty laugh. "Okay, then," I said, taking the soldier's hand again. "We'll report back as soon as we can. Maybe we'll even call you from Central Command!" More chuckles. "Hey, you haven't by any chance got a hip flask?" But now my little soldier's face fell: he wasn't even sure of the nature of his inadequacy to this request. Should've known better than to ask of him, or Balkan either, anything in any way *hip*.

Nevertheless, we got my revolver back, a free escort past their cordon, and a glance at their map, which I was inclined to trust about as far as it extended into actual space, say eighteen or twenty inches. Still, I flattered it with my intense scrutiny. Then I saluted my soldier and he just about fainted with gratitude. "Come on," I said, giddying-up Balkan, who wanted to linger and gape at the marginally well-orchestrated maneuvers the Brat Patrol were conducting on the far side of the spine. "Isn't Don Rondelay's Retreat just off that fork up ahead?"

I actually recognized the spot not thanks to the soldier's map but due to this being a stretch where for no reason I could imagine various souls had seen fit over the years to tie the laces of their old sneakers together and fling the resulting sneaker-bolo upwards so it wound around the high rafters of the spine, too high for anyone without a hook-and-ladder to cut them down. There must have been a hundred pairs of sneakers dangling there. Who knows how these things get started? But I digress.

"Uh, who?" said Balkan, a little disingenuously, I thought.

"Come on, Balkan. Don Rondelay's. It's a famous orgy, longest-running in the whole ribs and shoulders, maybe the whole shape. Don't say *he's* gone belly-up, you'll break my heart—" *Belly-up* a mild pun here, since *why not* at an orgy, right? Wasted on Balkan, needless to say.

"No, it's still there," said Balkan nervously, catching me by the arm. "I don't see why we ought to—uh, Mr. F, there's nothing we need from that place—"

"Don't you think we ought to make a report?"

"Oh, no, Mr. F." Very serious now. "I've seen reports. Activities there are at an, um, complete standstill. I mean, no one goes in or out anymore—"

"No in or out? *That's* hard to believe." Pathetic, the shallows of my amusement.

"There's nothing, uh, likely nothing to be learned or gained or, uh, discerned—"

"Maybe something to be un-learned, though. For the discerning. That's you and me, Balkan." I tugged out of his grasp and lurched in the direction my old spider-sense told me the door to Don Rondelay's Grotto was still to be found. Balkan hurried after me.

Actually, *standstill* sort of described the situation inside. What I'd remembered as a quite spontaneous and free-form day-and-night grope-a-thon— sprawled, pulsing, inelegant bodies rich in scars, tattoos and cellulite, spilled wine, cigarettes stubbed in smeared plates of soft cheese and onion dip, weird fricative sounds and snorts of laughter—seemed to have hardened into precious ritual, a scene as glossy and predictable as silicone. Up front a buffed "master" in a zipper-mask, leather loincloth, and hood snapped a whip to direct waxy six-foot women in G-strings in a series of theatricalized, slow-motion tableau—coy lesbian scenes, silk-ribbon bondage, lollipop-sucking, mock-horse-and-rider play—for the benefit of passive watchers of both sexes. In the second room a woman in a quasi-military outfit directed a group of young men in a new-recruit fantasy, including strip-searches, buzz haircuts, and light hazing. It was all dimly, tastefully perverted and as remote from a good, crunchy, nutritional orgy as I could fathom. The drill-sergeant woman spotted something in Balkan the minute we walked in, crooked her finger at him, and he fell in place with her other recruits, bugging his eyes at me helplessly. I waved dismissively—*knock yourself out!*—and pressed through to the next room, certain there had to be a bar somewhere, or at least a concession stand.

The inner sanctum was the most ludicrous of all. Lit by strobe a group of women writhed and danced while men seated at a long glass counter watched not the bodies but their shadows reflected on the far wall. The place was perfumed and soundtracked like a mausoleum. Old Don Rondelay himself presided, the fat corrupt toad—I was oddly pleased to see him leaning there in the back doorway smoking a stogie and surely counting real and imaginary gold behind his half-lidded eyes. The more things change, etc. And tending bar at the counter was none other than Highball.

He quit polishing a shaker long enough to salute me. "Long time no see."

I mimed crawling out of the desert to an oasis, choked at my neck to stress the urgency of my thirst.

He poured a shot onto rocks, kept pouring until it was two shots. "This still your usual?"

"Not usual enough."

"What brings you around?"

"Fight with the wife." I slugged at his—well, Don Rondelay's—good bourbon, savored the heat of it.

"Wanna talk about it?"

"What's to talk about? It's the typical stuff: son's no good, third eye might hold secret of the universe but conversely might not, man's gotta do what a man's gotta do—"

"I more than understand."

I raised my glass to him. "Is it just me, or is this place a little on the, uh, formal and regimented side all of a sudden?"

"Tell me about it."

"This militia craze that's sweeping The Young People of the Shape Today knows no bounds."

"Martial memory," agreed Highball.

"What the fuck is *that* supposed to mean?" I said, surprised by the ragged claw of anger that went scuttling across the floor of my gut. "I mean, memory of *what?*" Or had he said *Marshall Memory*—like a hero in a Western?

He held up both his hands. "I just work here."

"Mr. F, Mr. F—" It was Balkan. He came in to the bar area bare-chested, clutching his shirt in one hand and his unfastened belt in the other, running like a kid who'd screwed up at potty.

"Hello, Balkan."

He buckled his belt and straightened up, saluted me with the free hand. "Mr. F, they've got one of those red phones I was telling you about, a line to Central Command—"

"Well hey ho," I said. "Guess we ought to check it out." I drained my glass, plunked it in front of Highball. "What do I owe you?"

Highball just raised his chin at Don Rondelay, who nodded back and lifted his cigar to me. "You're good here," said Highball. "Don't be a stranger."

The red phone was mounted in a cubby off the second room. It was in use. Another guy about Balkan's age was curled around it with his back to us, speaking in a low, gummy voice. "Yeah, that's it," he said. "God, you sound so good, I wish I could see you right now. You know what I'd do if we were in the *same room* right now?" His hand, I noticed at this point, was jammed into his pants. The guy was having better fun than the actual patrons of the orgy, far as I could tell. Balkan stood staring dumbly, tugging his shirt back into place, waiting for me to decode his world for him yet again.

"I think this particular red phone has been corrupted," I told Balkan. "Must be something about the milieu. Context wins as usual."

"Maybe we ought to, you know, seize control of the phone," he said weakly.

"Too soon for any sort of seizure," I told him. "We're still in fly-in-the-ointment mode here, gathering info. *Recognizance,* remember?"

"Ointment?"

"It's where flies go when they're sick of the wall," I said. "C'mon, I think I know where we can get another dose."

Navigating by the compass of our bender, Balkan and I made our way through the upper chest, honoring as many of my old haunts as still stood, otherwise cadging booze from sentries running nutrient fabricators on behalf of a variety of local despots, tinhorn regional sheriffs and faintly charismatic cult figureheads. Everywhere troops of one definition or another were massing, being drummed into this or that obscure warlike fervor, whether under the guise of religious or scientific or merely paranoiac revelations provided by up-to-the-minute reports and rumors from the various competing eyes. We ducked conscription, needless to say. No credit to Balkan, but we ducked. Our bender petered just as we found our way into the neck, and it was there we finally crashed for a bout of R&R at a flop run by missionaries of the nuclear-shelter-theory persuasion. *"We must strive to comport ourselves in a manner befitting the privileged survivors of worldwide catastrophe,"* was the texture of hair-shirt they were selling at the interminable lectures we and fifteen or so other stragglers had to sit through just to get a free bowl of their lousy cream of nothing soup. *"We owe this to the many millions who perished when we alone were granted salvation in the shelter of the shape. Those perished and their countless generations of children who will never be. We live for them and we must live as they would have had us live,"* never imagining of course that the countless unborn billions might have enjoyed a snort of hootch now and again. They were pushing something on the order of a twelve-step program for the spirit within and the shape without, and we put up with their ranting and blather for as long as it took to get a couple of squares and a ten-hour snooze on their narrow cots.

It was as I ground the nuggets of sleep out of the corners of my eyes and began to anticipate scaring up a hair of the dog that I found the eldest and most bearded and sanctimonious of those long-robed propagandists waiting by the side of my cot.

"May I ask you a question, sir?"

"You already have."

"In these great times, sir, it is a shame and a sorrow to see a man of your stature and accomplishment leading a band of two on so paltry a mission as that which brought you to our door."

"True, it's barely more than a paltry-raid," I agreed.

He didn't acknowledge the pun. "In these great times of ours a man of your particular rank, sir, should lead a sizable and righteous legion. The shape is much in need of the leadership you could provide."

"Could would should," I said. "Maybe I've got a higher calling, a family duty. Blood being thicker than hoo-ha."

"Family values are not incompatible with our views, sir."

I noticed now that Balkan was gone from his cot, along with the others who'd slept in our room. The goofballs had arranged for this to be a private confab. "Make your point," I said.

"The surface temperature is cooling, Geiger readings indicate a readiness for human reoccupation. This will be a task for the greatest among us—despite how they may have consoled or distracted themselves through the years of waiting for that which we all must desire—"

"Yah, yah, what Geiger counter, whose readings?"

"Before we share our secrets, sir, we need a sign of good faith from you. In our circle there are those—

though I am not among them—who fear you already represent some other faction, that you feign your inconstant ways and are with us now on some mission of infiltration."

"Hey, far be it from me to *feign*." I winced at myself. The guy would have me babbling pentameter any minute now. "Why don't you just spill it? If I don't get with your program I promise to drown your precious secrets along with the rest of the stuff I'm pickling."

He lowered his voice to a biblical *basso profundo*. "Let us show you our eye."

I whistled. "Boy, you're some heavy dudes. Just a local outfit working the gutter patrol, that's what I took you for. Deep *in mufti*, I guess. Your own eye, wow. That a right or a left eye?"

"It is the *one true eye*, sir."

"And it's yours."

"We have exclusive rights, yes sir."

"And you think so damn much of me—wow."

"Would you come with us, sir." Another of the elders stepped out of the corridor, and I saw them trade nods.

"My man Balkan is coming along, isn't he?"

"We would prefer you visit alone. Your companion is busy playing video games at the moment, sir, and I doubt he'll notice your absence."

They had it all figured, a bit too neat for me. "Tell

boys had struck a deal—likely for food, protection, who knew what else—with a clique of young nuns who controlled the eye. And I do mean controlled. The first met us in a small antechamber, the entrance of which had been masked by a large and stinking garbage dumpster. She wore a heavy ring of keys on a chain around her waist and a thick black cape and cowl, but when she turned her head I could see she wasn't more than eighteen or twenty, with bright red cheeks, a dewy chin. And the cheeks were active, jawing, working at something: I thought at first some sort of speaking-in-tongues subvocalizing, then realized—bubble gum. She keyed open the door at the rear of the chamber and we entered a long, desolate corridor, lit with candles, where two more nuns—one for each of us now, I tried not to shame myself by thinking—waited silently. The corridor was hot and nearly airless, the smell of garbage overwhelming, and I wondered if the nun's zone had suffered some breakdown of atmosphere processing, coolant leakage, maybe a complete loss of power. It would explain the candles, and the nuns' dependence on the dopes from downstairs. Plus air this dead and hot wasn't something women in woolly cowls likely suffered solely for aesthetic or ascetic purposes. On the whole, I thought, an unpromising spot for an ontology-shattering eye. But maybe I'd find temporary employment with the nuns as a garbage hider—my only true calling, after all. They sure could use one.

There was a bit more rigmarole and a whole bunch more nuns, a majority of them also chewing gum under their cowls, before we were shown into an equally muggy circular chamber, lit again with candles, the ceiling studded with hundreds of tiny reflective stickers in the shapes of stars and moons and ringed planets, that old headshop dorm-room staple. The chamber's stepped tile floor inclined towards a thirty-foot-high black curtain, which veiled the furthest section of curved wall: presumably the you-guessed-it. When the curtain was parted I took another slug of Old Overholt, thought *an ice cube, my kingdom for an ice cube,* and stepped up for a look.

It was pretty impressive. A shoreline horizon stretched out, sand and ocean, distant jetty of rocks, and the shock, the vaulting endless shock of sky. And right in the center of the frame—for it was a frame, most artfully composed—a vast figurative sculpture, a titan in rotting green copper, jutted at an impossible angle from its place half-swallowed in the sand. The figure was a totem of a woman in a robe and a spiked headdress. She bore a torch to heaven, only it was now tipped away to point at the edge of sky and water instead. Seabirds wheeled and clouds tumbled ever so slightly in the sky, but this panorama was a tape loop or I was a monkey's commanding officer. The nuns were sure to draw the curtain before much longer. I didn't give them the chance.

"Boys, you've been rooked," I said.

The nuns at either end of the curtain only bowed their heads. The elders who'd brought me here stepped closer, and the three of us, all sweating like pigs, peered through the eye at the epic scene. It was a thing of beauty, really, if you took it for what it was: installation art. I wondered what genius was behind the fallen grandeur of that statue in the sand—it somehow didn't seem the handiwork of an eighteen year-old nun. I could imagine if I let myself that the statue was another shape, that it too was jammed full of people wondering if they were alone and that we were lodged in the sand of the same beach just a few hundred yards away. That perhaps Balkan was half-right, we were an intergenerational starship, one of a vast fleet, only not in space at all. We'd long-ago landed on this beach and merely didn't have the sense to open the airlock and look around. The statue was dignified and stupid—its uprightness didn't matter in the least, not tilted sideways as it was. It made me think of me and Marianne, us trying to raise a kid in the subburrows as though life in the shape could make sense, as though we could raise a torch to the sky, and instead having it go all to hell. It also nagged at me, that image, seemed something I should but didn't want to remember, the name of the statue, the movie the still was from. And that in turn reminded me of the fact itself that there were *things I didn't wish to remember.*

Whichever way I contemplated it the statue image was dire and sad and made me feel the poison of years in my aching bones and I stood and lost myself in it for a moment, nursing the whisky, feeling sorry for myself and the poor credulous missionaries who'd come to worship this balderdash.

"Fleeced, by a flock of nuns," I said. "And you probably ought to be *de*frocked, for that matter. I mean, come now, gentlemen. You can even see the pixels." I mopped the sweat off my neck with my sleeve, and turned my back on the eye.

"The cynic sees only what the cynic allows himself to see," said the first elder, he of the bedside ministrations.

"Whatever. We're barely halfway up the neck in the first place. This couldn't be an eye, no matter what movie was playing. It's more along the lines of a *tracheotomy*." I offered the bottle around, figuring they could use it about now. No takers. "All right, ladies, get us out of here. But first permit me to use your john, if you would."

"I like that, oh yeah, so I tell you to do it faster, and you do it faster, and I like it faster, but then you tell me to go slow, you don't want to come yet, so I do go slow—"

The red phone in the spiral staircase was occupied too. "Awful lot of people having *phone sex* with Central Command these days," I said to Balkan, just jerking his chain.

He'd been in a lousy mood ever since I pulled him out of the rec room and told him what he'd missed, the nun-tended eye, the lady in the sand. I made up some shit too, about how I'd pulled my revolver and blasted a hole in the screen they were claiming as a vista, and how the *inky, airless depths of interstellar space* came whooshing in and sucked away all the oxygen and gravity so we were bouncing around like human motes and one of the missionaries flew through the hole in the screen and I had to rescue a bunch of the screaming nuns single-handedly—Balkan would swallow just about anything, and he was, understandably, a bit miffed to have spent the whole time playing *Frogger.* He didn't say anything and we continued up the spiral stairs until the moans of the soldier on the red phone were out of earshot.

Balkan knew his way back after all, to the eye in question. *Left eye,* I believe it was in retrospect, though I got a bit turned around myself, and blacked out for a spell in the jaw and nose. I remember something about pulling Balkan out of a bar fight and it wasn't Balkan, it was some other guy instead and he was about to sock me when I pulled my rusty trusty revolver and then Balkan came out and we ran—something about that. What's less deeply shrouded in mental fog is the Buddhist commune in the bridge of the nose where they fed and bathed and reclothed us—I'd pissed my pants at some point, the shame centering in not being able to say exactly when or how long I'd been going around like that. For a religious order the Buddhists were pleasantly free with their rice wine and so we got a nice relaunch though we were dressed now in saffron robes and our heads were shaved. But shortly thereafter Balkan ran into some brethren from his own militia—the rump boys, or "liver" gang, as they preferred to believe—and we exchanged our robes for militia garb. Balkan got his corporal's stripes back, and they fitted me in a Napoleonic jacket with epaulets and felt buttons. I looked like Marlon Brando in *Mutiny on the Apocalypse Now*.

We'd just drained our last bottle of the monk's sake when we rounded a corner and found it. The line to get in for a glimpse of Balkan's favored eye stretched down a vast corridor towards the cheek, too long to see the head of the line from the end, and there were people camped out who'd plainly been there for weeks, playing chess, sleeping on cardboard boxes, changing diapers on squalling infants, taking turns on a red phone. Concessionaires, missionaries, recruiters and soapbox propagandists were working the crowd, selling cigarettes, transcendence, death-by-glory and other ideologies.

"Did you wait on this when you got in before?" I asked Balkan.

"It—it moves quicker than it looks," he said with embarrassment.

"Holy hell," I said. "That's harshing my mellow, bigtime." The closer we got to finding Dennis the more looped I needed to be. I was at a nice pitch right at that moment and shacking up with the squatters was out of the question. "Let's go." I pushed up through the crowd milling at the end of the line and started for the front. Balkan followed, as we snaked along the line drawing stares and jeers and come-ons of a few different flavors. We found, surprise surprise, a pair of young soldiers manning the door at the top of the line.

"Where's Dennis?" I whispered to Balkan.

"Inside," he said. "You'll see."

"Alrighty then." I inhaled deeply and drew out of myself a deep-chested command-baritone. Albeit aloft on drunkard's breath. "Private, seal this door behind us. We're going in."

The soldiers widened their eyes, but stood firm.

Balkan showed mettle for once. "Do you understand who you're talking to?" he demanded, poking a finger into one sentry's chest.

"Sir, yes sir!"

"Good, then. So let's get with the program."

"Now just *wait one minute there, buster.*" This from behind us, a woman's voice. At the head of the line, a young couple dressed in hippie paisley and with identical greasy bangs, him sheepish, projecting desperate hopes of non-involvement, she fiery with indignation. "We've been waiting here for *three days,* along with a whole lot of other people. Who says you can just barrel up here and skip the line?"

"It's a—military matter," I said weakly, hating to hear myself begin playing that particular card with a civilian. The militia boys got a thrill out of it, I knew, but I didn't really like the way it made me feel inside.

"Who *cares?*" said the hippie chick. "We *all* want to see the eye. We all have our *very important* reasons."

"Military-important is different from regular-important," whined Balkan, his moment of gravitas passed.

"Fuck this," I said, feeling suddenly impatient and criminal, not really into procedure *at all.* I whipped out my revolver, hoped she couldn't spot at close range the frozen-with-rust trigger under my finger.

Whether for that reason or some other, she wasn't impressed. She pulled a half-wilted daisy out of her hair and slipped it neatly into the barrel, where it drooped impotently. We all stood in a semi-circle around this astonishment of a woman and stared at the limp flower in dumb silence. Her boyfriend looked like he wanted to tackle her to the ground himself.

One of the sentries took a leaf from Balkan's book and pointed a finger at her. "DO YOU KNOW WHO YOU'RE DEALING WITH, YOUNG LADY?" He being, just incidentally, as young as the girl, or younger.

"Of course," she said. "Everybody knows who he is. He's a garbage hider who used to be important, but he isn't anymore. Why don't you go back to your little bowel in the subbowels, garbage hider, and leave the rest of us alone?"

"Please, let's not get gratuitously ugly," I said. "That's *burrow* in the *sub-burrows*." This being among the more important euphemisms in my existence, and I'm sure I don't have to explain why.

A nascent hubbub began rippling back through the line behind the couple, and I knew it was time to cut this short. "C'mon, Balkan." I turned to the girl one last time. "Age before beauty, baby. We won't be long."

The proscenium was a little more persuasive this time, a tad more on the scale of one of the shape's original, actual eyes: a planetarium-sized oak-lined hall with a series of recessed conference tables and a waist-high polished brass rail running along the front of the eye's opening. The room was lit gently by green-shaded desk lamps on the tables in the rear. Three tourists stood at the rail gazing into the depths silently—all I could see from here was blackness, possibly inky but I couldn't say yet for sure—but from the back of the room, in the conference area, I heard a murmur of prayer or discussion which echoed majestically across the vaulted ceiling. If it wasn't a true eye it was a copy with a lot of integrity, that much was sure. It stirred something in me, some faint lost sense of grandeur or stature, an impulse to assert my place in the shape with pride, rather than to huddle and cope in some marginal, contemptible organ.

"Where's Dennis?" I whispered again.

Balkan nodded in the direction of the conference tables, the murmurs.

I found him sitting cross-legged on one of the inlaid-wood tables, with a bowl of coins in front of him, chanting lightly, his eyes rolled back, slits of lid showing only white.

"Dennis?"

"*Dad?*" He jerked to attention, saintly posture abandoned.

"Yeah, kid, it's me." I reached out, but an impulse to clap him sharply on the ear became tender in mid-air, and I riffled his lopsided haircut instead.

"Wow." He looked, saw Balkan, scoped the room to be sure, I suppose, that we weren't spearheading some invasion of troops into his holy chamber.

"They said you were coming, that you'd been seen marching around."

"Who said?"

"Lots of people. You lost all your hair?"

"Shaved."

"Wow. I guess you're gearing up for a really major operation, huh?"

"I don't know about that, son. My head was shaved by some Buddhists."

"Oh." I could see that one didn't exactly compute, but he let it go. Probably thought it was classified information, a code-word or some such. "So have you looked at the eye, dad? It's so beautiful."

"It looks beautiful, son. I'd like to go have a closer look."

"You should. Then, I don't know—you and Balkan want to go get something to eat or something?" He was so humble and unrebellious I wanted to weep. I would rather he threw his idiot philosophy in my face, just for the display of backbone. Instead he was an amiable noodle.

All I said was: "Sounds great, Dennis."

I nodded at Balkan. He stayed with Dennis and I went to the rail.

Black, absolute. That's what I saw at first, and so I leaned in closer to the glass, expecting something more. There was nothing more. It was seamless, glintless, fearless, indifferent black—no stars. The curve of the glass cornea reflected the faint light, the green lampshades and oak-paneled tones of the room behind me, my own wondering expression, gin-blistered nose, gleaming pate. The black on the other side of the glass was either infinitely flat or infinitely deep. There was no point of reference, no glimmer or ripple or scratch in the black to give a cue either way. It might have been the bottom of the ocean floor, and on the other side of the glass a million pounds of pressurized water waiting to flood the shape and drown us and return us to our primordial origins. It might have been the vast pupil of God's or Big Brother's unblinking eye. It might have been a vidscreen turned off. Just about the only thing it couldn't have been was the inky depths of interstellar space, because last I checked stellar involved stars.

Dennis didn't balk at leaving with us. Seeing them walk ahead of me, Balkan in his ill-fitting uniform and Dennis padding along in bare feet, the two of them talking about whatever, I remembered Dennis and Balkan playing together as eight or nine year-olds and it just about broke my heart, thinking of their innocence then and, really, still. Their impressionable hearts might now be all invested in grim, cryptic yearnings, in strained, over-serious postures—yet it was innocence nevertheless, innocence all the more so. I wanted nothing worse at that moment than never to see boys stripped of their boyishness, never to see them led into battle as I myself had once been led. Never to see it. And never to lead.

"I'd like to help you find the third eye, Dad," said Dennis humbly when we got away from the maelstrom of that corridor, the sorry population waiting in line to stare into the utterly black eye, waiting to prop up whatever screwed-up hope or lousy, third-hand theory had brought them there in the first place.

"We'll see, Dennis." I was fantasizing about a vodka gimlet at that moment, actually, and my silly brain was thinking *gimlet-eyed, maybe find a gimlet in the eye*—"If there even is one, which I'm still not persuaded—"

That, as it happened, was when Balkan snapped. We were strolling past a soldier on a red phone, just another kid of course, but he was saying something like "So my tongue is licking the line between your navel—" and Balkan ripped the receiver from his grasp and knocked the kid onto the floor.

"Hello? Hello? Is this Central Command?" Balkan's eyes were wild with the release of long-deferred frustration. "IS THIS CENTRAL COMMAND?"

The kid got up out of the dust of the floor, his lower lip sticking out, his expression all pouty at being bullied away from the phone, hand still in his pants. "Vamoose," I told him. "Scram. Here—" I held out my hand to Balkan. "Gimme."

"Okay, Mr. F. They're not saying anything. I don't understand."

I took the receiver. "Hello?" I said. There was silence, then a crabbed, squawking voice said "Hello?"

"Is this, uh, Central Command?"

"Ceeentraaal Commaaaand," screeched the voice. "Do me, baby."

"I'm sorry?"

"*Oh* yeah," said Central Command. "*That's* it. That's *it*. *That's it, that's it!*"

I figured: what the hell. "So, is there a third eye?"

"Touch my third eye! That's it, baby! Oh yeah! Aaaawwk!" This last was less than persuasively orgasmic, more a strangled bleat.

Irked, I hung up the phone, then shrugged helplessly at Balkan. "Central Command is, uh, out of order." Balkan furrowed his brow.

"Dad?" Dennis had been watching our little skit with calm detachment, his head cocked ever so slightly, like a puppy's.

"Yes?"

"When I said I wanted to help you find the third eye—?" Dennis had somewhere developed that excruciating habit of finishing ordinary statements with an insecure tone of questioning, as though he'd spent his childhood having the word *NO!* bellowed at him. Which emphatically wasn't the case. I'd raised that kid like I was running an egg-and-spoon race through a minefield, and he was the egg.

"Yes?"

"I *meant* I might really be able to help you find it."

Two operatives had sought Dennis out at his place in the eye, and after giving him alms for a few chants— "I did a really good one with the syllables *UR* and *OW*" was his memorable digression—told him they wanted to talk. They said they knew he was interested in the question of the third eye, though how they'd come by this information Dennis couldn't explain. They imparted to him an understanding of how the body/brain barrier was pretty much impermeable, *with one exception,* and then explained that they wished to entrust him with coordinates of this crucial exception, the reason being that another operative would be coming by, a fellow who would need to be told how to *permeate the impermeable,* in order to make a top-secret visit to the shape's brain, which was where the third eye was hidden—atop the brain. They wished for Dennis to function as their contact, hiding in plain sight as he already was (in the form of a contemptible, hebephrenic beggar). These operatives, whom Dennis, when asked to characterize them, declared *"actually really nice guys,"* displaying an impoverishment of both self-protective instincts and descriptive powers that left his dear father appalled, led him bodily from the eye to the place where we now stood, he and I and Balkan, in front of a hole-in-the-wall restaurant in the upper nose called *Not Burn Down.* The smell coming out of *Not Burn Down* suggested the name was either abject plea or foolhardy provocation.

The specialty of the house was *rind with curd,* but their gimmick was this: the rind had been formed into the shapes of various animals, then hung from giant meathooks in a gruesome line along the front of the grill. The animals were all out of scale, the pig and duck and lamb and cow and ostrich the same size, but there was one incongruous showpiece, a large horse. Well, not larger than a *real horse,* considerably smaller in fact, but in the cramped space of the storefront and by comparison to the other rind-creatures it loomed. The grillmaster stood behind the fuming, sputtering fire and slivered chunks off the animals showily, with a long curved knife and what appeared to be a miniature Satan's pitchfork. TRY ARE MIXXE GRILLE! shouted a smoke-stained banner on the far wall, and the few disconsolate customers all seemed to be doing that, their plates heaped with various chunks of blackened rind and sides of curd—though from appearances the pig-shaped-rind and the horse-shaped-rind and all the rest were the same proteinous gluten through and through.

"This way," whispered Dennis, and he led us to the back of the restaurant, towards the door to a darkened back room. The grillmaster stepped up and barred the way, brandishing his knife and skewer in an X across his chest to suggest the possibility of some foul, utensil-based martial art.

Hothead that I am—or possibly the smell was getting to me—I pulled my revolver. "Out of the way, or your animals get it," I growled, putting my gun's muzzle to the rind-horse's ear.

"No, no, High Commander," said the grillmaster, bowing deeply. "I could never stand in your way. I merely wished to say it is a great honor to have you come here. We have all waited for this day with hope and trembling." He finished the bow with a flourish, and like a toreador waved his skewer to indicate our way past him. "Please, sir."

Shamed into silence, I lowered my weapon, and we went inside.

The dumbwaiter was barely big enough for the three of us. Balkan sat in my lap, and Dennis's elbow lodged in my ear. The grillmaster waved us farewell, closed the tiny door, and flipped the lever that propelled us upwards. Crammed into the dark little cubicle with Balkan and Dennis I fantasized we were being injected into the shape's brain, and I wondered then if we were a depressant or a euphoric, a virus or a cure. I was, in other words, beginning to entertain that we were *something,* that our homely little band was, however uncanny, a more-than-negligible force or irritant within the shape.

"Mr. F?"

"Yes, Balkan."

"You're a good man, Mr. F. I just wanted to say that."

"Thank you, Balkan."

We thumped to a stop at the top of its shaft and tumbled out, like circus clowns from a little import. We'd outletted in an empty corridor, one chilly and clean and almost blindingly brightly lit. We were surrounded by a tightly wound team of shock troops even as we were uncrimping our joints, rubbing our eyes, and smoothing our rumpled uniforms—hearing the click of an automatic safety lifting I looked up to find four of them kneeling with us in their sights while another four came hurtling and grunting—"Go, go, go, go!"—around a corner, smoothly unholstering as they fell in behind the others. I had to admire their real polish and precision—these were something more than the fantasizing househusbands and weekend reservists roaming the bulk of the shape lately. They knew how to stay out of one another's lines of fire, a rarer distinction than you'd think. Balkan tumbled into a elaborate pose of surrender, elbows-to-knees, head ducked, fingers laced behind his neck, so efficiently I wondered if he'd been rehearsing it. Dennis opened his hands like Al Jolson singing "Mammy" and began to chant, "Ah, da, ma, aaah, daaah, maaah." Oh, what a goose he was. Me, I chucked my rusty firearm so it slid spinning on the tile to a place at the toe of the team captain's boot.

"We come in pieces," I said, nodding to include my idiot company. "All marbles not necessarily included."

"Up!" said the team leader, waving his piece at Balkan and Dennis, who was kowtowing as he keened.

"Is *that* how we got here?" I smacked my forehead in mock disbelief. But Mr. Severity wasn't going to get baited into a lot of curlicued patter. Having proved his verbal chops with a single syllable, he and his troop made do with pantomime thereafter, wedging their firearms into our backs and force-marching us in single file down the corridor in the direction from which they'd come.

I was separated from Balkan and Dennis at the half-open door of an executive office, the last in a long series of offices we'd passed. Balkan and Dennis were hustled away with the majority of the troops, and I was nudged inside.

"Farbur, is that *you?*"

I squinted at the man behind the desk, not fully believing my eyes. He wore the same dapper uniform as his troops, but nothing could cover the roguish, insouciant expression, or the drunkard's blossoming veins that networked his cheeks and nose.

"Peabody? *Dutton* Peabody?"

"Well, well. Have a seat, Farbur. *Take a load off.* Boys, feast your eyes on none other than Henry Farbur. I've been waiting a long time for this day!"

"I thought you were a *newspaperman,* Peabody. In the left hind shank, if memory serves." It *didn't,* but hey. "How'd you end up in command up here?" Somewhere back behind the misty veils of time, Dutton Peabody had run a fairly good tabloid on mimeograph paper, called *The Shinbone Star.* Daily sheet—good crime blotter, lively personals section, editorials yellow only in ways I approved.

"Times change, old soldier. Times change and men adapt."

I couldn't disagree. "Too bad it's not the other way around, though, isn't it?"

"You may have a point there, Farbur. You may well have a point. Boys, let me have a word with Mr. Farbur here alone, if you would." Of course he drew a nice bottle of amber stuff out of his desk before his troopers had even shut the door.

"To—service."

I drank to his toast, dimly ashamed at the implicit comparison between his crisp uniform and crack troops and my goonish costume, my slapstick stooges. The liquid fire went down good, though, chasing away meemies of various kinds, the eerie fateful echoes that had been building up around me in the past days. It was high time to shake them off. If an old joker like Peabody could thrive in this sober atmosphere of obligation and rearmament, then I ought to be able to wiggle through, just as long as I kept nicely oiled. I drained the glass.

"This is just what the doctor ordered," I joshed. "And the distracter, and the defector, and the disjointer. They all ordered the same thing."

"You sound like a man with something on his chest." He poured me another.

"Oh, for a little while there I was afraid I'd lost sight of the objective—that being: *to lose sight of the objective.* But here's the antidote." I hoisted the glass, winked broadly, slurped away a mouthful.

"If I follow you, it sounds like there might actually be two objectives."

"Yup, that's one way to look at it. Two objectives: Preparedness and, uh, its opposite. One-hundred-percent vigilant wakeful readiness is our first priority. Second priority: blissful, slumbering-idiot complacency." I was giddy with my own wit, drunk on it as much as on the scotch. *Oh, self-love and self-involvement, sweet priceless obfuscators of grim reality!*

As if reading my mind, Peabody said, "First objective, deception, second objective, self-deception."

"Deception?" I played possum. "I don't know from

deception. Who were we trying to deceive?" I knocked back the rest of the shot. "Man, that's killer shit."

"You're like the guy in the joke, Henry. You forgot what you drink to forget."

"On the good days I forget. I was having a bad one just now."

He lowered his voice. "Your bad day isn't over, General Farbur." I looked up from my glass and caught him staring. Peabody and I ought to have been two old salts knocking a few back, getting three sheets to the thin wind coming out of the air ducts. But now I noticed his own drink was untouched.

Don't drag me back, I wanted to warn him. Instead I said, "I resigned my commission. I'm nobody's general, haven't been for twenty-odd years. I'm a garbage hider."

"You really need to take a look at the eye, Henry." Now he drank.

Peabody and I stepped back out into the brightly lit corridor, into an atmosphere of muted pomp. A dozen of his troopers were lined up at attention along the wall, and Balkan and Dennis stood with them. They'd each been issued clean uniforms and they looked, I had to admit, pretty dapper, pretty upright. Things were changing, wheels were turning, whether I chose to acknowledge them or not. Peabody stepped up to Balkan and Dennis and patted them each lightly on the cheek, and they stood inert and proud, eyes fixed on some middle distance, some imaginary battle, waiting to be told to be at ease. Dennis was tall in his new boots.

"They're going to make great soldiers, Henry," said Peabody. "We'll train them in, start while you're upstairs. In no time they'll be damn fine fighting men."

"Dennis?" I said.

"Sir? I mean, Dad?"

"Is this what you want?"

"Uh, yes Dad sir."

Now I wished to hear him chant again, hear him boast of the nirvana of intoned syllables. Yes-Dad-sir would do fine, I thought: yesdadsir, yesdadsir. I wanted to hear it and throw a coin in his cup myself. I wanted to see him in bare feet, scuttling dorkishly. I thought of Marianne, how she'd commanded me to *bring him back*.

"All right, kid. We'll—we'll talk about it when I get back."

Peabody dismissed the unit and they marched away. I let myself be led across the corridor, to a locked stairwell door. Peabody keyed it open, then pressed the key into my palm. Like the floor of offices, the stairwell was clean and spare and flooded with light. There wasn't a trace of human life, not a whiff, not an echo.

"We'll be waiting to hear from you, Henry," said Peabody, clapping my shoulder.

"Okeydokey," I said in a moron voice. I wished feebly to defuse the air of immanence, of severity. But *okeydokey* didn't make any impression on Peabody at all.

"These men are positively aching for your command. You only have to say the word."

I was at a loss.

"Hey, almost forgot—here." Peabody reached into his interior breast pocket, emerged with a slim hip flask, in filigreed silver. I dimly recognized the elaborately decorated monogram: H-A-F. Henry Allan Farbur. I lifted it out of his hands. It sloshed promisingly.

"I've been saving it for you. Smell."

I took a sniff. It was good stuff, very good stuff.

"We know how you work, Henry. I don't have to say any more, do I? Welcome back."

I screwed the cap back, my fingers savoring the neatly worked metal, the elegance of the flask. I slipped it into the pocket of my Napoleon jacket.

"I—I think I'll go see the eye now, Dutton."

"You do that." He winked. "We're not going anywhere without you."

At the top of the stairwell was another locked door. It took the key Peabody had slipped me.

There were thirty of the birds—I counted. Large white parrots, football-sized, with a plume of feathers at the neck. *Thick-billed parrots*—I was fairly certain of the breed name. The birds stood on mounts in cubicles in the vast white office, each wearing a headset with a vocal mic curved to meet the front of its bill. A spiral cord trailed from each headset to a phone on the cubicle desks, which were otherwise clean, though the cubicle floors were heaped with little white-green pyramids of birdshit. The odor in the room was thin and intense, like ammonia, and the sounds the parrots made formed a cacophonous squalling wall-of-sound:

"Put it in there! Put it in there! It's good in there! Oh yeah!"

"I'm coming, I'm coming, I'm coming. I'm come. I'm come!"

"Aaaawwrrk! So big!"

"Do I like it? Do I like it? Ak. Ak. Shreeee. Do I? Do I? Shreee."

"Okay. Touch my thigh. Higher. Higher. Thigher. There. Here. Here-here. Oop! There-there. Higher—"

And so on. Other parrots seemed for the moment only to be listening, turning their plumed heads this way and that as they considered the odd noises coming over their headphones.

I moved through the office, ignoring the birds as best I could. At the other end of the room there was a white door marked PRIVATE, and under PRIVATE someone had scrawled with a magic marker *third eye third eye set me free.* I tried the handle. The door was unlocked.

It was nothing like the other eyes I'd seen, had none of the grandeur of those several likely bogus and the two or three possibly legitimate contenders for right or left eye, no curved, vaulted retinal space, no darkened chamber, no ritual aspect whatsoever. It was an office with a window, and the window wasn't very large. A modest telescope stood on a tripod at the window, aimed downwards. And it was otherwise an ordinary office: shelves, desk, chair, gray short-hair carpet. There were a few styrofoam cups of cold coffee dregs and a couple of mustard-stained sandwich wrappings on the desk. I went to the window.

From the angle and view I understood that this office was high in the shade of the left ear. If I leaned in close to the window I could see the curve of the left cheek and brow to my right, a slight bulge of neck to my left. My view straight down was partly occluded by the prominent muscle of the left forelimb, which formed a semicircle spanning the width of that downward view—and like a fat man trying to spot his shoetips beneath the swell of his own middle I could just see a nubbin of the left hoof poking out far below that semicircle of muscle. Cheek, brow, neck, shoulder, hoof—that was all I could see of the shape itself, but it was more than enough.

It was what I saw beyond the shape itself that made my mission clear at last, at long last. At long last I understood and recalled as I sat in the chair at the desk and I focused the telescope and took it all in, surveyed the terrain, the field of future battle. Below the limit of the sky ran a perimeter of highway, where passenger cars and commercial trucks full of food and alcohol and durable goods and other treasure whirred ceaselessly past, borne to families in sprawling suburbs blanketed with unimaginable lawns, their lives a throbbing feast of waste and complacency. Distant smokestacks tooted poison into a pale blue sky. In the unseeable distance beyond the highway and the smokestacks men golfed, died, farted, called their secretaries on speakerphones. All lay beyond that boundary where trucks full of ripening avocadoes and bottles of Zinfandel pulsed and rattled to their destinations.

Nearer to the shape was another matter. Everything between that eight-lane horizon line of highway and the hoof of the shape where it met the pavement straight below me was included in a vast gated park, a compound full of gaily painted gingerbread buildings incoherently bedecked with onion domes, doric columns, and porthole windows. Between the buildings zipped little three-wheeled carts with fringed tops, threading lanes amidst Tilt-a-Whirl rides and coin-speckled fountains and themed shape, *this shape*—and I saw postcards and T-shirts too, icons rendered soft and silly for mass consumption. They'd given the shape goggling eyeballs and buck teeth and an endearing scruff of hair in the place of its majestic fearsome eyes and grim-set mouth and noble mane. I saw it and I felt a stir of triumph—we'd lulled them, the morons had actually believed us, they'd wheeled our giant horse into their turf and built this shit factory around it and begun charging admission like it was Graceland, a cute impotent relic, they were so grievously corrupt that they were wearing our grand and mighty instrument of war *on their T-shirts* and they were in the palms of our hands at last. I couldn't hide from myself anymore now, I was awake, awake and sober (though pulling hard on my hip flask, believe me) and full of martial hate and pride and only a little weariness, a trace of regret perhaps—but fuck it, really. Why shouldn't old soldiers get off their lawn chairs and lead pale young men into battle? Did I mean to spend the rest of my days scraping shreds of protein off the grill? Why shouldn't Balkan's bluff get called, why shouldn't Dennis figure out *what really makes his old man tick?* Why shouldn't nearly thirty years of lying in wait, of losing ourselves in distraction and dissolution, of losing sight of our rhyme and reason, our deep-embedded programming, come to a grand and glorious end as we spill out of hiding and smite them high and hard, finally *take it to the hole.* Why shouldn't they get what's coming? I mean, what the fuck was I so afraid of?

The whole shape had been clamoring for my leadership, I saw now—boys had begun to march and salute, to feel the pulse of war without knowing why, and those priestly rumors of *landing* or *returning to the surface* were all part of the same long-slumbering, now-waking impulse to fulfill our destiny. Operatives had told Dennis that he'd have to lead another operative to the third eye—hey, that other operative was me!

I began by strangling and plucking and making a stew out of thirty filthy-mouthed thick-billed parrots. A task considerably rougher on my sloth-softened hands than you might imagine. But those birds weren't bad eating, not bad at all.

Then I started answering the phones.